STRAIGHT RED?

When not losing is this important, do the odds really matter?

Darrell McDonald

Dedicated to my purpose:
Locks, Little tic and One toot';
forever you will be my number one

100% of profits from the sale of this
book will be donated to Sarcoma UK, a
national charity that funds vital research
and offers information and support to
anyone affected by sarcoma cancer.

.

The greatness of a person is not in how much wealth they acquire, but in their integrity and ability to affect those around them with positivity

- Bob Marley

Original quote amended to be more inclusive

1.

I'm at a football match and am wearing red and white in support of West Brighton City although I don't really follow them. Redhill also normally wear red, but they are in their away colours today: a yucky pale yellow and snotty green. They have a strange name (the Island Club bit), legend has it, they were originally called Redhill FC, but their owner had a dream about the club being really successful; they were strong and determined, and all their opponents feared them. He tried, as we all do with vague dreams, to gain some understanding of how they became that way, but he struggled to recall many of the details. The only thing he definitely remembered was seeing characters in Mandarin; 狡猾的 (which loosely translates to the word 'devious'). He became obsessed with countries that spoke Mandarin. As you can imagine, getting any information on these countries back in the day, when the alphabet isn't even the same, was not easy. He spent hours and hours at libraries researching; Taiwan - nothing, Singapore - nothing, Hong Kong - nothing, all before looking into China. Why he didn't start, there given the 10-figure population, will remain a mystery. It was there that he finally found a place called 'Redhill Island'. "Can't be a coincidence", he thought. So like a person possessed, he could think of nothing else than this other Redhill six thousand miles away. He felt sure this Redhill held the key to success - he must visit.

He couldn't find any direct flights to Redhill Island but there was an option with a change in Beijing onto a chartered plane, total cost: £1,711. You may consider that a large sum to satisfy some curiosity brought on by a period of rapid eye movement, but not for this impulsive club owner whose impetuous nature is probably only matched by the depth of his pockets. There was no debate – trip booked.

Arriving at his destination, a shadowy and mysterious island, with traps and mini-sinkholes, he found few roads but many winding and tortuous paths to walk. Some of the signs were in English and Mandarin, and one stood out to him above the others: "Beware of" and then a poorly painted picture of a hyena. "This is it!" he thought. "We must be like the devious, scavenging hyena and TAKE what we want! The hyena doesn't ask before it takes; it is feared by its prey; it is a predator. Get enough conniving hyenas together and they'll take from the all-powerful, king of the jungle, Lion!"

His trip stopped right there, at that moment. If it isn't obvious, here we have a really devil-may-care guy who just 'does'. His mission was complete, his team need to be cunning and devious like the hyena - it matched with the Mandarin word he saw in his dream - it all fits. Despite the fact that it turned out Redhill Island wasn't an island at all, but a peninsula, the new name stuck and along with it, a new philosophy for the club: henceforth, Redhill Island Football Club would be the name and playing without scruples would be the game. And as 'prophesied', the new club, shortened to Redhill Island Club, with the nickname RIC, started to win, due to the name change of course(!)...although no-one was fooled that it was actually the dirty tactics philosophy that was leading to the better win rate.

Given the opportunity, they'd attack you while you slept, they'd mess with your food, use mind games, and sap your energy. They'd kick you when the ref wasn't looking: put simply, they bully their way to victory. Redhill are so caught up with tearing down their opponent, so focused on embodying their club 'spirit', that I don't even get why they want to win - do they even want to? It feels like they're so focused on being the villain, that they've forgotten it was a means to an end. The actual goal was to be more successful, not just to embody the devious hyena. Nowadays, they would choose for one of their players to get sent off if it would hurt the other team, like deliberately injuring the opposition's star striker whether this improved their chances of victory or not. It certainly feels like their only ambition is to destroy, that total destruction is *their* view of victory.

Redhill's opponents today are West Brighton City, Redhill's biggest rivals. I honestly can't tell you why; kit's odd. Typically, rivalry stems from being in the same area, but distance-wise, the teams are not that close: about 50 miles apart. I mean, Crawley Town FC are much closer, only 5 minutes down the road. With them, there is rivalry, but nothing like with Brighton who Redhill seem to hate more than anyone else. Maybe it stems from the giant causeway between their philosophies. After all, philosophies are our values, and, if held deeply enough, they can shape our very purpose for existing. Without values, why even be, why even live? It boils down to a very simple, yet hard to answer, 3-letter word: the **why**.

Brighton are competitive but play fairly. They will shake your hand after the match, no matter the outcome. They won't trash-talk, and if they had their way, there would be sporting respect; a 'may the best team win' mentality shown by everyone. They are a team in every sense of the word. Yes, they have star players with their individual strengths, but they play together. No one is trying to seek glory for themselves, no egos: rather they strive for collective achievement. This is exactly the same off the pitch; they know they are part of something bigger than the club, they are about being great role models for all, being active in the local community with activities ranging from park clean-up days to tackling anti-social behaviour, and having an even bigger impact with their pioneering sustainability initiatives. They work together to make a better environment. Every single person associated with the club including players, staff, sponsors, even caterers, must buy into this mission to positively impact all, and into their 'for the greater good' mindset, with no exceptions! And this approach attracts fans, not that their style of play isn't entertaining, but their true passion for positive progress is just infectious.

Anyway, enough about the teams. This match is different. I'm at a stadium for the first time in a long time. I want to blame something or someone for that but, to be fair, it's all on me. I like spending time at home; give me Netflix, Deliveroo and a low APR credit card and I'm golden. I maybe got too used to that, and so started going out less. But today is different – I'm out! I have an amazing view, pretty much bang on the halfway line, second row! It's one of those days where it's hot enough to leave your coat at home. I really feel cold easily, so this is a big deal for me.

Today is about watching a massive game, live, in person – something I realise I've really missed. When I worked in the Sport industry, I took this for granted – I'd be picky about what I attended – I won't do that again. I have to watch history happen – there are no replays, there is no "Alexa, pause TV", while I go for a wee. This is going to take place right in front of my eyes, now, and once only. I yearn to be able to say, "I was there", as all true sports fans do. But even though I'm conscious of all of that, today still feels strange, unfamiliar - I can't put my finger on it… it's sort of… surreal. I've even come on my own which is weird, have I ever done that before? That's got to be what's making it feel unusual.

This game is key, it's about survival for Brighton but the bookies have Redhill as massive favourites. If Brighton lose, they are relegated, their fight is over, but if they manage to draw or win against all odds, they get all that comes with staying in the top league, they survive for another season - this game means something! But Redhill would like nothing more than to be the cause of Brighton's downfall.

The team sheet is announced. Whilst Redhill fans greet every Brighton player's name with boos, Brighton show their respect with gentle applause for their opponents, and huge roars for their own players - especially Harry Ope and Neville Nia, their star players.

The ref blows the whistle to give all the opportunity to take a moment of silence to mark the passing of an ex-Brighton player, Gary Nelson. He was loved as much on the pitch as off, he played a big part in the ethics of the club, starting with his Elf Christmas movie family day screening on the big stadium screen, now in its 10th year, a staple part of the community calendar. Given what Redhill players and fans are like, what happened next completely shocked me: no, Redhill players didn't start shouting and booing, instead every single person in that stadium was absolutely silent, including the obnoxious Redhill fans, right until the whistle blew for a second time - not a peep. Wow! #ShockedEmoji

The players move to their starting positions.

The match starts.

2.

I'm in a doctor's office, or more accurately, a therapist's office - Dr. Lee's office. I don't remember how I got here, but it's my weekly opportunity to deal with some issues I have about my weight. My arm feels cold and wet and 'ouch' it's like a pin pricked me.

"Please do go on", I hear. Oh, I've drifted again, I'm not in the room. "Sorry, repeat the question", I say guiltily.

"You were telling me what happened."

The room I'm in feels very modern and expensive, but not at all intimidating. I find the pictures on the walls very calming: gentle seas and relaxing landscapes, minimal and elegant – my kind of style, if I had the money. There is a desk, but the doctor is sitting adjacent to me, with a solid wood coffee table equidistant to us both - no old magazines, just clear and clutter-free. Three walls are white with the fourth floor-to-ceiling glass. One of the white walls has a mixture of pictures of smiling people and accreditation certificates. I'm not sure how high up we are, maybe 10 floors, but there is a magnificent view of a river. This is a comfortable, but expensive place.

Sam, as Dr. Lee prefers to be called, is tall, calm, and confident. As with most therapists, they employ a nice, monotone, soothing voice, which just makes you feel safe. I tell the rather immaculately dressed doctor that I have a problem; that my dreams are so vivid at the moment that I'm struggling... I hesitate. I'm scared that I'll come across as crazy. Their reassuring voice responds, "if it's easier to talk with your eyes closed so you feel less on the spot, that's fine - just relax and breathe". I take a comforting deep breath, close my eyes, and begin:

"My problem... I have a..." I stutter.

"Just take your time..."

Is this really a safe place for me to say what I'm thinking and feeling? After all, I'm not the most open and confident person - I'm a right introverted hermit, apart from when I'm with V (more about her later). I take one more big inhale... slowly... breathe out, and then I start:

Picture it: Sicily, it was 2018. I'm on holiday and should be having a great time but instead it's an okay time. Just *okay* because the trip is not quite what we had pictured – it's nice, it's warm, it's quiet, but you know that feeling you get when the image you've built up in your head in anticipation just isn't what you end up with. Like when you take a cheat-day and order a massive greasy take-away only when you eat it, for it to be cold and unsatisfying. And then you have the guilt of eating junk as your 'just desserts'. Well, maybe that's over-egging it, so I'll just say what happened. I thought I had booked a hotel for this awesome trip to

Sicily when actually it's more of an Air BnB style. I thought people would do things for us: make the bed, make the breakfast, make the cocktails, and we'd be left to just make the memories. Well, we had to make everything – that's not a fun relaxing holiday, that's just everyday life in a different postcode.

The voices in my head say it's not for us, we should cut our losses and relocate to an actual hotel – after all, it's only money – this time is priceless. So that's what we did: we packed up, posted the key back in its combination lock and moved to a massively overpriced hotel with great ratings to fulfil our desire to relax... well, at least that was the plan.

More about the hotel later, but what is weird is that whilst I remember the trip really well: the first place had a dog called

Oliver and a freezing pool because they don't heat pools in Sicily especially in March, I cannot find any pictures on my phone from the trip... bizarre as I always take some pictures when I'm away, even if I have to delete my chess app to free up storage space.

"The problem, doctor, is I keep having these crazy vivid dreams - they feel so real. I struggle sometimes to know if I'm recalling memories or if it's one of those dreams." Did I really go to Sicily?

3.

I suddenly realise I'm back at the game. No one has scored yet but Brighton look scared... like they already feel battered by fear about what is to come – it's intense remembering the trauma from previous encounters as well as the stories from others' who have had battles with Redhill. No one looks forward to playing these thugs. You may be the fittest athlete, the sharpest reader of the game, you may be an expert on the opposition's playing style, you may have eaten the right foods, taken all the right supplements, be the most confident of teams against anyone else, but EVERYONE's confidence is shaken by the thought of battling with Redhill - bar none (Vinnie Jones would be proud). Even those who have achieved victories against them still get nervous when there is even the possibility of playing them again. Time and time again, the fear alone is the cause of downfall for many opponents - Redhill know it and they love it!

I have ref link (for those who don't know, ref link is an earpiece that allows you to hear the voice of the referee) but there is some static. I mess with the dials trying to fix it, the frequency must be wrong or something. Just as I start to get up to go back to the booth to get a replacement, I hear a voice - ah, I must have sorted it. I sit back down. What's weird is, I can see the ref but he isn't talking and yet, I can hear voices - so who can I hear? I start scanning around to see if it looks like one of the other officials. It isn't, instead it's Redhill's coach: what the??

He's talking to a sub: "Johnny - didn't you sleep with number 8's girlfriend?" Johnny is their captain, the conductor of the way they play, so it's strange that he's on the bench. He has two jobs: one, ensuring anyone joining the team understands their style of *play,* and for those who don't, making sure they are swiftly, shall we say, physically encouraged to leave the club, i.e. going full ahwooga on them. And two, coordinating the 'non-sporting activities' for games. The oversized, built like a brick-sh$t house, Johnny replies: "I did, a few times, but it was terrible, not worth remembering". "Yeah, well, make number 8 remember - that will throw him off his game".

Number 8 is Neville Nia, Brighton's captain. Random fact, the name Nia is of Swahili origin meaning 'goal, or purpose' - very fitting as through his role as captain, he like Johnny, makes sure the clubs ethics are understood by any player joining the squad. Neville takes his responsibility very seriously - it's his purpose. He is a role model, almost like the wise grandad of the club. I have no doubt that when he retires from playing, he will move into the boardroom and continue the great work.

Given RIC's under-handed style of play, Johnny as captain clearly has no moral code or boundaries. "I actually did worse, I kinda started leaving stuff at theirs... small things to make him wonder...makes him think, "hmm something just feels off", but he can't quite put his finger on what. I'll put socks in his pants drawer, I'll use his protein powder up, I even added a series link to his TiVo for that 90's show "Cheaters" - it must be bothering him so much!"

Wow, people will actually turn the lives of others upside down for their own personal gain. Johnny is effectively seeping into Nia's life, tearing it down from the inside, all just to later make an ugly appearance when useful: disgusting! All for a fricking game!

Johnny is subbed on and immediately finds Nia. I can't hear the words, but Nia's body language is loud and obvious. He looks broken, devastated by whatever he is being told - his mind is elsewhere and at that moment, Brighton concede - it's 1-0 to Redhill.

The whole Redhill subs bench starts cheering and shouting hysterically, so loudly that I reactively rip the ref link out of my ear.

4.

"**A**re you ok? You drifted then," says the doctor. "You were talking about Sicily, kind of like Sophia from The Golden Girls". I did say it like that; her famous "picture it" phrase - maybe that's the sign that it was a dream. In any case I continue to recount details of my trip.

The hotel was lovely, all set in 6 acres

of land which is uncommon in Sicily - so much space to roam. It was light and modern, and overlooked a beautiful harbour. The service was first class. An abundance of leisure facilities at our doorstep, including a spa, gym, bowling alley, cinema, night club... the list goes on. Oh, and our very own butler, although I prefer the term *concierge*. Butler just feels a bit colonial. The food was delicious, and just the right amount to not feel you'd eaten too much, but just enough to feel satisfied. I have a problem with over-indulging sometimes.

Unfortunately, the lovely hotel with its high ceilings, ocean views and premium alcohol was just finishing some renovation works (that must be why it was available at such short notice). Loads of loud noises - it was so bad that the hotel got all guests special headphones to partially cover up the noise. Stefano our concierge yells, "IT'S JUST FOR ONE MORE HOUR", trying to be heard over the constant banging as he handed them out. I'm certain mine were busted, I mean they work, but all I can hear (apart from the banging noises) is Katy Perry - Katy Perry's greatest hits on loop - no DJ Optic mega mix, no Earth, Wind & Fire, no Pharrell... just KP and it's not even greatest hits - it's 3 songs: *Firework*, that one with Snoop that I can't remember the name of and *Roar*. I actually like *Roar*; it has a great 'keep on fighting' message:

'I've got the eye of the Tiger, a fighter, dancing through the fire'

Oh, and *Firework*, that has an even stronger inner positivity message. Katy Perry was quoted say:

'I really believe that people have a spark to be a firework..A lot of the times it's only us that's standing in the way of reaching our goals, fulfilling our destinies, being the best version of who we possibly can be'

Anyway, finally, after 48 minutes, the noise stops. I have somehow fallen asleep lying flat on my back on a sun lounger and am gently awoken by Stefano who oddly has a shoddy uniform; it looks more like chef whites or a nurse's scrubs than a quality hotel's concierge uniform - I don't remember noticing that before. He helps me to sit-up and then gently removes my headphones... ahhh, the calm, the quiet - THIS is what I wanted. And it continued like this for the remaining 4 days of the trip - peace, good food and some local vino rosso for good measure. The noise from the overrunning renovation works actually gave me a much stronger appreciation for the calm, the still, the silence. Our decision to move, validated!

"Do you feel you need more serenity in your everyday life?" asks Dr. Lee.

5.

I'm lucky to live on a road where the neighbours are very friendly and chatty, although this can be a challenge if I'm late for a train and no matter how many times I say, "I'm late..." or "I'm just on my way to...", there are still a few minutes of chit chat to get through before leaving the street. I jest really because actually if everyone ignored me, I'd feel like the kid picked last at school for football. I'm massively grateful for our neighbours.

In one of these chats, I'm told that Mr. Kew from number 55 has the flu. I'm running late for a Slimming World meeting so have to dash off (for real) but I tell myself to check in on him on my way home. I finish Slimming World feeling particularly positive this week and so rather than get myself a curry, which is my normal "I'm taking this seriously except when I want a curry" approach. I stop by Cook and find a couple of stick-in-the-oven healthy meals and go and knock on Mr. Kew's door.

I wait patiently as he makes his way to the door. He opens it cautiously, as someone would who hasn't had visitors in a while. His family live far away and although I do visit to keep him company from time to time, it's not every week.

"I've got some food if you're hungry?" He welcomes me in, and we go to the kitchen. We end up talking loads while we wait for our supper to be ready. He challenges me on my ambitions - I make up some nonsense about wanting to be a retail store manager but he sees right through me. He has prodded me on this before but today he is much more direct, almost as if he wants to give me advice to change me now rather than wait.

"You would like to be an architect, right?" he says very sternly, with an intense, no flinching, stare. "But you don't WANT to be, you don't crave it - why not??". I mean, come on old man, I'm just trying to help you out and you're making me feel like a loser.

I actually do really, really want to be an architect - I have sketchbook upon sketchbook full of amazing ideas but I can't afford to take time to study: I've got bills to pay (and debt) but I'm too embarrassed to admit that's why.

A news alert goes off on my phone - the perfect distraction. "Oh, can you believe it, another Fixed Penalty Notice for our PM?" I say out loud, hoping to divert the conversation away from my life's failings. "I've lost count of how many now - I bet he's expensing them," scoffs Mr. Kew. From then on, the conversation is a bit more light-hearted and after a few hours, with a full belly, I say goodbye. As I'm heading out I suggest, "How about we make this a weekly thing after my Slimming World meetings? He nods, happy about the suggestion, but clearly a little tired from all the chatting.

We keep up our new weekly routine, only difference being, each week he digs a little deeper into my ambitions, but I don't mind - he is right, it's not about ambition or drive or desire - it's purely financial. I start to open up and even show him some of my sketches and designs and, in doing so, his view of me seems to change. It kind of goes from 'poor boy I'm trying to lift up' to 'wow, this kid just needs some support as he has a real talent'.

Sadly, the flu turns into something more serious and Mr. K passes. Maybe he knew it was more serious but didn't want to let on. Months later, I get a call from a solicitor regarding Mr. K's will. I'm in it with the note:

Use this to stop the excuses and follow your

passion.

He's left me the money I need to get out of debt, which can free me up to go back to uni and finish what I started, to continue my journey to becoming an architect and leave stacking shelves at W.H. Smith behind.

All very thoughtful from my friend at number 55.

Bam, Bam, Bam goes my door!! It's so loud, I think it's the police...

"Can I call you back?" I hastily say to the solicitor and hang up.

"My father's money?? You scammed my father out of what should be mine?!! I'm gonna break this door down and rip out ya throat!!"

I obviously do NOT open the door. My

3 months of self-defence class combined with this body is not helping stop any angry person from kicking my head in. I sit on the floor with my back to the door. That is one thing my body is good for - it's not easy to move. I just yell back, "what do you mean? Who are you?"

"YOU. KNOW. WHO. I. AM!"

Given he said 'father' while hurling abuse at me, I can only assume it's Mr. K's son. When I said his family lived far away, what I meant was, his son was in prison and so was unable to visit. He was found guilty of drug possession, which was relatively minor. Attacking the arresting officers on the other hand is what ultimately got him 3-5 years of care at HMP Brixton. When that was, I don't know but clearly Barnaby Kew was out.

This is not someone I can have a chat with, he will not listen to reason, he's like the non-empathetic terminator and he thinks I've screwed him over. He doesn't hear or want to know the facts. He doesn't care that while he's been inside, I've been helping out and popping in, and all with only positive intentions. And actually, I'm proud of that, whatever Barnaby thinks.

I helped and was written into the will - I didn't plan for that or ask for it, I helped because it was the right thing to do, but the feeling that people might think I'm scamming, it hurts, it hurts deeply. I was trying to help, and it has been turned into something nasty. This feeling is awful. It makes me feel sick, more than feel... I throw up... I throw up right there at my front door. I throw up again. Barnaby hears this and you'd think he'd at least check I was alright. Of course, he doesn't, but I guess he must feel some level of pity, as he leaves. I run to the toilet. I throw up again and again until my body just heaves. I feel hot and sweaty; physically drained and vulnerable - it feels like I'm being poisoned.

"So, to answer your question doctor, yes, I could do with more serenity in my life."

"What sort of things do you do to facilitate it? What are your coping mechanisms to feel calmer? Was Mr. K one of those for you?"

6.

I'm obese. I say I don't care, but I do. And it's a vicious cycle: I eat for comfort; I don't want to exercise as it hurts and I think I look stupid, so I eat and be jolly and basically brush it off. How long has my weight been an issue? Do you know... I don't know, I feel like it's always just been a part of me. Maybe V knows (I said I'd come back to her). Venus, who I call V for short, is my friend. She is super-smart, ultra-kind and almost as funny as me: my very best friend (apart from food). I feel safe and calm with her.

I give her a call, like I would normally - we do our general catch-up on yesterday's events as we talk EVERYDAY. I don't know how we find things to talk about. However, this time my tone is different - I want to be serious. I want a real answer.

"V? We both know I'm overweight - please don't try and be nice and say I'm not." "I wasn't going to," she abruptly replies in her no-nonsense way. "What I want to know is *when* do you think it started?" I've known V since primary school. We've been besties since then. She's a TV presenter, cool, right? And I'm a W.H. Smith Assistant Manager... well, working towards becoming one, at least that's what they keep telling me, *sigh*.

"You really don't know?" She says in a firm yet confused way as if the answer is so obvious this must be some kind of test or trick. Flash! A light bulb goes off in my mind, it's so bright, so clear that I don't understand how I had put it out of my mind so much that I couldn't remember. I was repressing trauma - how strange and yet fascinating. The light released the memory in a millisecond, of course I know why. It feels so cliché to say, but I was bullied.

The bully, Ricardo, used to threaten me to get my dinner money, but as I didn't have much because I tended to have packed lunch - sandwiches, crisps and chocolate, he would take my chocolate, a bit like the Highway Rat. You'd think the frequent chocolate robberies would stop me eating chocolate, but it had quite the opposite effect. I always made sure I had chocolate in my bag, just in case. On the days when I came home and the chocolate was still there in my bag, I felt great, I felt safe. I had gone another day without being bullied and tormented; I hadn't been a victim on those days. And when I ate that (saved) chocolate, the positive feelings intensified. If you repeat and repeat and repeat something, good or bad, the habit forms, the link becomes stronger, and in this case, my brain cannot help but connect chocolate (and other foods) with happy feelings of safety and security. This eventually led to an addiction, and then an obsession. I can't even use the defence that I didn't know what was happening – I knew my eating was getting out of hand, but it felt so good. I am ashamed to say that I feel like I allowed the bullying to continue because it justified my chocolate over-indulgence – it was my excuse. I never fought back, I just took the abuse – no prevention, just enjoyed the cure!

And eating wasn't the only thing I did to address the feelings of helplessness and lack of control - I got addicted to Mortal Kombat and virtually every other combat-fighting-beat-'em-up video game out there. I'd play hour after hour, by myself, in my room. I lived for earning high rankings, but even more, I craved unlocking characters and new levels which required winning fights in unique ways each time - you have to play the same level over and over and over again, winning with different combinations each time. Game-makers clearly know how to keep you *engaged*.

It was so bad. I remember this time when

I had to make a choice between staying warm or playing games. When I still lived at home, we didn't have much money, I say that like I have Sultan-level riches now, I clearly don't. But back then, it was a different level. Our electricity was on a prepay meter and one day it needed topping up.

Mum had taken the prepay card so she could add credit on her way home from work. I was 2 wins away from finally completing my 20th no-kicks allowed win in Mortal Kombat II. That is how you unlock the Optic Mindful Warrior character. However, the electricity was low and it was getting cold as the sun was setting. I remember going and checking the meter: 17p remaining. I had been in this position before - if the electricity goes off, the console will go off and I'll have to start my 20 wins all over again. At this pont, I had been attempting this for hours and up to this point, the most in a row I had achieved was 14. I was really close but it was really getting cold. The choice to be made was clear - be warm or be a hero! You know the pretend kind of hero on a game that only true gamers will understand:

'The geeks will inherit the Earth'

So, what did I do? I turned off all the lights, grabbed a duvet to wrap around myself, and I played on!

You can see that I have an addictive personality, but I knew it had to stop. That was the old me, and this is the changing me.

V and I have spoken for hours about my eating habits. She's tried her best to get me to understand that school and the bully are behind us, so I don't need these coping mechanisms anymore – they are habits that need breaking. I don't know how but she was the one who got me signed up to Slimming World – but even then, I'm not taking it too seriously. She realises it's about love – that I've stopped loving myself... that my spark is diminishing, my light is retreating – I'm spending more and more time alone. It was great when Mr. K was still here– he was turning that around but since he's been gone, I've started to regress. "I'm coming over" she says and slams the phone down. As I move the phone from my ear, a little too quickly, I tweak my neck - it's not massively painful, just a bit stiff. I start to make my way to the kitchen to get some ice for it. Having my head at a slightly odd angle is disorientating me a little, to the point

I slow down my pace and sort of shuffle along.

"Ding dong". With the shock of the bell, I turn my head instinctively quickly and feel a sharp pinch in my neck as if I've woken up from an uncomfortable night's sleep which resulted in a crooked neck - I've now made it worse. I cautiously get up, trying not to make any sudden movements that may exacerbate it further. I open the door; V looks furious. She starts, "I'm going to talk and you're going to listen.."

She goes on to dish out not just tough love but real-talk, reality hurts, and "things ya mumma shoulda told ya", all in one huge outburst. Most of it actually goes in... it all summarises into "Love YOU...love yourself," she tells me – fight back! It's so terrifyingly shocking that I breakdown with emotion. I start crying there on the spot like a patient who's just received a horrific prognosis. She realises her message has got through to me, and gives me a hug. Our closeness means she too is feeling my pain.

The hug is long... and necessary, and then V prepares to leave. "I know that was a bit tough for both of us," V says in a very soft, empathetic voice. "I'll give you some space". I'm still a bit out of it from the shock-talk. She heads for the door, opens it and then tries to pull it shut gently as if that will help sustain my fragile emotional state, but it's a bit stiff. She pulls a bit harder but doesn't quite get the job done... so she gives a final massive tug which slams it shut hard - BLAM!

The door slam shocks me out of my trance-like state...

7.

Ah, I'm back at the therapist's office. But something is off. I look at the white walls... well, grey walls... the diplomas seem a little different, and why have they removed the walnut coffee table? Wait a minute, there are 4 walls - I could have sworn one was floor to ceiling glass, but now there is just a grubby rectangular window with a window lock - not very calming. I make my way over to the window to take a closer look. "Where's the water gone?" I say whilst gazing out. "Are we in a different room to normal?"

"What do you mean?" is the confused response. I turn around, "you know...-" I stop abruptly as I realise this is *not* Dr. Lee. "I'm so sorry, I must be in the wrong room."

"No, you're in the right place. Are you ok?" I'm both stunned and confused in equal measure. I gaze around the room a bit more, this is definitely not an expensive therapist's office. There are no smiling faces of positivity on the wall, but there are certificates. I move closer to check the name on the accreditations. I don't expect them to say Dr. Sam Lee but that was not the biggest revelation... I read slowly in my mind:

'Cymru, University of Wales, Cardiff. It is hereby certified that Andrew Billingham is awarded a postgraduate master's degree in the field of Oncology'

Oncology? Wait, what? As in cancer? As in I'm going to die???! I have just been dealt the body's equivalent of a *straight red card.*

Oh wow, what is going on? WHERE AM I?? I begin to pant, fast shallow breaths, my heartbeat thinks I'm sprinting and has proceeded to accelerate faster and faster. Now, hopefully this is one of those dreams that I'm struggling to distinguish from reality, it just has to be.

"I think it would be better if you sat down." I hear in a slightly concerned tone from what must be Mr. Billingham. I slowly walk over to a chair unsteadily like a deer who's just been born. As I do, I spot my reflection in a mirror. I take a back step to have a better look. I don't recognise the image I see before me. My face is swollen and chubby like an MMA post-fight photo, and my hair, or what's left of it, looks very patchy. I start to slowly shift my gaze downwards... I have a plaster on my neck, a really small one like you'd get after a vaccination... I keep going. Chest looks normal, although man-boobs are absent. Arms... in my left arm I see a cannula. And my torso... it's, well, thin - not obese, not a before picture for a protein shake advert. Oh, this is too much - that is not me... is it?

I quickly find a seat and bend forward with my head between my legs, my hands on my face, and start whispering to myself repeatedly: "what is going on?" I'm so confused. Mr. Billingham takes a seat too, and slowly brings me up to speed.

He tells me I am at the Royal Marsden Hospital; I have been having treatment for a soft-tissue sarcoma cancer, which is extremely rare. "No, no, no, NO!,"rapidly spews from my mouth. "Someone is playing a trick, I'm just here for therapy - where is Dr. Lee? I don't even know who you are!"

"Who? There is no Dr. Lee here. I've seen this only a handful of times before; 'selective confabulation'."

"Selective conf-what?"

"Selective confabulation - it's when a patient generates false memories or realities, which they are completely convinced are real. The situation they find themselves in is so scary, so huge, that the mind finds creative and unusual ways to deal with the stress, to avoid the harsh reality."

Could it be that's what I'm doing now? All the things I discussed with Dr. Lee - what about Sicily, Mr. Kew - what about the game? *This* has to be a dream, not that. Of course, if this were a dream, it would definitely try to convince me that *it* was reality and everything else was just a figment of my imagination.

"Why don't you tell me about these *stories* and we can take it from there," he says in that comforting tone that Dr. Lee used...I think. I take a deep breath, preparing to describe my memories, definitely my *memories*. My breathing begins to slow as I try to recount details.

Sometimes dreams are a manifestation of our thoughts, hopes, worries, I'm told in a comforting but almost patronising way, although I'm probably being sensitive given that from my perspective, I've just appeared in a random doctor's office to be greeted with the news that I have cancer, when I just wanted some gentle counselling to reduce my waist size (although thinking about it, it is odd that I could afford Dr. Lee).

"As you go through them, try to consider if anything unusual stands out about any of these situations? That might help clarify if it's a real memory or not, as just like dreams, confabulations tend to include oddities. If you remember, for example, jumping off Waterloo Bridge and not getting hurt, that one's probably not a memory, but also look for other small subtleties, like objects in unusual places: keys in the fridge, your red car is blue, that sort of thing."

Before I start, I look down at my arm again and immediately have a flashback to Dr. Lee's office where I had that cold, wet feeling before a sharp scratch... I pause. My mind is suddenly getting clearer. That 'pin pricked me feeling' was very random at the time, but the feeling was in the exact same place on my arm as the incision point of the cannula I'm now staring at in my arm - I begin to realise...

Sicily, those loud banging noises with the headphones playing Katy Perry - that was weird, and I can't find any photos of that trip. So much for subtle things to test reality, that was a big fat sign that it didn't happen. But what was it?

"What kind of banging noises?" enquires Dr. B. I do my very best to recreate the rhythmic sounds, I feel a bit like a failed beatboxer, but it's just good enough that he recognises it - "that sounds like an MRI scan - you've had those, and you always request Katy Perry to listen to."

That's it! It was the sound from the scanner, and as they are so loud, they give you headphones with music to drown it out a bit! Now that I realise these stories are just that - it all starts making sense - fricking confabulation - that's what this has all been??

I continue, next talking about Mr. Kew, the throwing up when Barnaby was threatening me, that was my body reacting to chemotherapy treatment, which essentially is a form of poisoning, it's very toxic.

That plaster on my neck, where I had that sudden pain, that's where they took cells for a biopsy...

And V, with her message to love myself. Now I think of it, since being diagnosed, I've taken it badly - I want to blame someone, something, anything. Before now, I mainly made good health choices: I was fairly active, didn't smoke, ate my vegetables - so why is this happening to me? I must have done something to deserve this! The message from Venus, now loud and clear, was to stop all that blame and start loving myself again - it's all making sense, my coping mechanism for my horrendous situation, these very wild fantasies. In the immortal words of Biggie (the Notorious B.I.G.):

'It was all a dream'

But what about the game? Was that odd? Definitely. The ref link thing, me being there on my own - all odd. So, wait, that means THIS is real? This sarcoma is in me. I have cancer and cancer is always serious. I find this realisation so shocking that I start to get dizzy as my heart begins to race again, and I pass out.

Now I see myself: I'm in a hospital bed. In the room are more medical staff than you'd think were needed for a simple fainting. To my left I see my rock-of-a-wife and beautiful kids. I'm not conscious but aware: I'm looking in my mind's eye – a sort of out-of-body experience. I'm hooked up to all sorts of monitoring machines. Then things start to happen, like when you have just woken up from a dream. Your mind hasn't quite clicked back into reality yet, but it's making its way there, slowly gaining more clarity and focus with each passing second - did I just dream the Dr. Billingham meeting? I still have the unanswered question of what does the game mean; or was *that* real?? I'm frantically trying to recall.

"His heart rate is rising..." yells a concerned nurse. The tempo of the staff in the room suddenly accelerates.

All of a sudden, my mind goes blank, calm and still.

...

... nothing

...

... quiet and empty.

...

A moment passes...

Who knows how long a moment is, but it felt like time didn't matter in THIS moment.

I blackout again.

❋ ❋ ❋

8.

I'm at the game. Brighton are not looking good. It has been largely one-sided so far but somehow, they are still only trailing by 1 goal. The ref has been pretty good all match but has made a massive error by not realising that Redhill are back to a full team after having had a player sent off about 20 minutes ago: RIC have brought on, not subbed on, but brought on, an extra player putting them back at 11! I never saw it happen but they definitely have more players on the pitch than they should - it's as if they are multiplying. Whether the ref should have noticed or not, there is no debate that it's plain cheating. How do they get away with being so sneaky... with their antics going undetected? How on earth can Brighton get something out of this game? They are massive underdogs which is only made worse by RIC's cheating.

I can hear the medical staff back in the hospital through my ref link. "It looks like he's giving up," says one nurse. Another replies: "Should we just make him comfortable?"

"NO!" yells my wife. "You do not know my husband; he is NOT done, he is NOT DONE". I've been frantically trying to understand why my mind created the game...now I know. This game is the manifestation of the battle my mind is having, it's against the odds and it is considering quitting - it's so hard. This game may not be happening physically, but it is every bit real in the sense that losing this game is losing the mental battle with cancer. I start to put the pieces of this psychological warfare together:

Redhill Island Club...

RIC...

Rare Incurable Cancer.

West Brighton City...

WBC...

White Blood Cells - the body's main defence mechanism to any illness or disease.

Redhill: sneaky, devious, hell bent on destruction, physically attack the opposition, even when they sleep. Cancer - same attributes.

Brighton: fair play, want harmony, protective of all, winning is not the objective, but improving the environment for all, is. White blood cells - same attributes.

The outcome of this game will directly affect my real fight with this horrendous disease - they are 100% connected.

I put my focus back to the game. WBC look dejected as do their fans. I decide to get a chant started, to produce some positivity into the players and the fans: I just start shouting "we've got Ope, we've got Ope, we've got Op-". I stop short as I look down at my team sheet and see Harry Ope's name... It's not written *Harry Ope*, they just put *H. Ope* - without the dot it kinda looks like the word *hope*. Of course, they need *hope* to win this!

The chant seems to be working; the players appear to be responding.

Brighton intercept a pass and go hard on the counter, passing the ball through the field towards RIC's goal. I'm not sure they've even had a shot on target yet. The ball gets to Nia at the edge of the box. Exactly the person you'd want to receive it in this situation. If he can get a little closer, he'll at least get a shot on target or maybe even go against the run of play and score. He dribbles left after a fake to the right and gets into the box. You can tell he only has shooting on his mind. He pulls his leg back like an archer about to fire, and, just as he's about to make contact with the ball, he is fouled from behind – the crowd gasp – it's not clear if Nia is injured seriously or if he'll be okay to continue: he needs a bit of Mr. Myagi's quick heal magic. The ref points to the penalty spot and issues Redhill's second red card of the day. This was typical RIC play: better to get sent off than allow Brighton the chance to score, akin to Luis Suarez in the 2010 World Cup – Ghana will never forgive him for that, ever! Nia, after receiving medical attention, seems ok to take the penalty. He takes a moment to compose himself. We're already out of time; we're ironically in the last minute of injury time - it's now or never to save WBC's season - to keep this mental battle going. Everything seems to be in slow motion. Nia walks back a few steps from the ball, takes a sharp intake of breath and breathes slowly out, and then begins his run up to the ball. He shoots but oh no, the keeper goes the right way and it's saved. In the milliseconds after the save, Redhill fans start to cheer... but a little prematurely, the keeper saves it but only by punching it to his left – right into the path of Ope who takes full advantage and lashes it back towards the goal – he scores from the rebound! It's 1-1, the draw they need. Just as quickly as Redhill fans started to cheer, silence descends on them. The whistle blows – it's over, Ope and Nia rose to the occasion and combined their efforts to get the result they needed! Ope and Nia, Hope and Purpose - those were the key, those ARE the key!

WBC have done it unexpectedly, against all the predictions, they found a way to beat the odds. Do stats matter? If 99% of teams lose that means 1%, no matter how small:

it means that **1% do NOT lose!**

EPILOGUE

I wrote this book for me, as an outlet for some of my thoughts and feelings, but I was encouraged to share the story with the hope of positively impacting others. If you do feel that reading my story has affected you in some way, then I've got more out of writing it than I could have hoped for! I would love to hear about the impact and *your* journey - get in touch:

Instagram: @StraightRedBook

Email: StraightRedBook@hotmail.com.

I have a rare *incurable* soft tissue sarcoma, which I have named RIC. I was diagnosed during COVID; on my 40th birthday in 2020. My primary tumour was discovered in my neck but, by the time they investigated it (thanks COVID), it had already spread to my lungs and brain, classifying me as a stage 4 patient. I've had chemotherapy and radiotherapy, and have been fortunate that it has reduced the size of my tumours, but they are still there, hence the *incurable* prognosis.

The news was tough to take but somehow, I found a way to change my mindset. I went from being a victim who thought it was, "Undeserving and unfair for cancer to strike me", to, "Well, why not me – someone *has* to get it". Pre-diagnosis, on the whole, I ate the right foods, didn't smoke, was fairly active and had little alcohol (apart from the odd V-festival style binge weekend). I was on the *safe* side of all the things you are told affect your chances of getting cancer. But yet, I was the unfortunate one sat in an oncologist's office being told I had months, rather than years, to live.

The change in my mindset came from two things: realising that I couldn't and cannot control everything, and knowing my **why.**

Firstly, the best chance I had of surviving was to focus on controlling the things I could. I have changed my diet, started meditating, and drink more water and less alcohol.

'I can't stop it from raining but
I can bring an umbrella'

In a weird way, Ric has helped me - I'm definitely getting more out of life than

I did before. I make sure I *live life* by turning up and being present. *'Live life'*, a phrase that my late father always used to say. You never know when life will take an unexpected turn... or when it will, to be blunt, just stop. His message was to embrace life **NOW** while you know that you can – really simple but powerful, thanks Pops.

Secondly, I realised my *why* and so put my wife and kids before everything. I log off when I say I'm going to, and I look forward to having my face painted by my 8-year-old to look like Black Panther. I look forward less to my 6-year-old suggesting we practise the box splits (which, for the record, he can do and I cannot!). I say yes to taking the kids on a 17-hour flight to make sure we all have an experience of a lifetime together on the other side of the world. And I say no to toxic relationships that, in the past, I would have just accepted and smiled along with excuses like, "It's because they are family" or "I've known them for years" – not anymore! What I do, who I do it with – there is a priority, and that priority is very important!

This fight against cancer is my battle, but not mine alone. I have a trail of positive, supportive and loving people behind me, with my wife Amy at the very front, having my back every step of the way. A lot of people say I'm inspirational and positive, which is very humbling to hear, and in some way is true, but my wife gets to see it all; the days when I am determined and feel like I can take on a bear, but also the days where I am weeping as I consider how my loved ones will be impacted if I lose. My fight will continue until I win,

or am incapable of battling anymore –
surrendering is NOT an option.

As I've said, I wrote this book for me, but
it is also to say thank you, a HUGE thank
you, to Amy. When we got married, I
gave her a thank you card rather than the
traditional husband or wife card because I
was grateful that she had chosen me to be
her life partner. We have been that since
the beginning: partners! We support each
other in bad times but, just as importantly,
we make sure we celebrate the good times
together too! I will forever be grateful to
have found and fallen in love with my best
friend and perfect soul mate!

ART

The cover art was created by Symone (Sym-hue.co.uk), a visual artist from South London who specialises in portraiture and figurative drawings and paintings.

She understood from the beginning that *Straight Red?* is a book filled with symbolism and so chose to create a piece that had a symbol at the very centre;

The Celtic Triskelion

 *The meaning of the Celtic Triskelion is seen as a symbol of strength and progress. As it appears to be moving, the Triskelion also represents the will to move forward and overcome adversity*

https://www.theirishroadtrip.com/celtic-symbols-and-meanings

Printed in Great Britain
by Amazon